A BUG TO HUG

BY THE SAME AUTHOR

A IS FOR ANYTHING:
An ABC Book of Pictures and Rhymes

A BUG TO HUG

by

KATHARINA BARRY

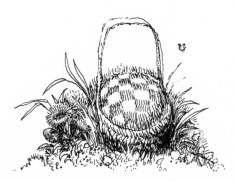

HARCOURT, BRACE & WORLD, INC.
NEW YORK

For Fruli

Would you like to hug a bug?

UGH!

Or would you rather bake a cake...

and make a mistake?

Would you like to rent a tent...

to an elephant?

Or would you rather share your chair...

with a grizzly bear?

Would you like a peck of speckles...

a hundred thousand freckles?

Or would you rather sail a mile down the Nile...

on a crocodile?

Would
you
like to
sing
higher ...

than
anyone
in
the
choir?

Or
would you
rather
take
an octopus...

on a bus?
(and make an enormous fuss!)

Would you like to invite a kangaroo...

for stew?

Or would you rather be defiant...

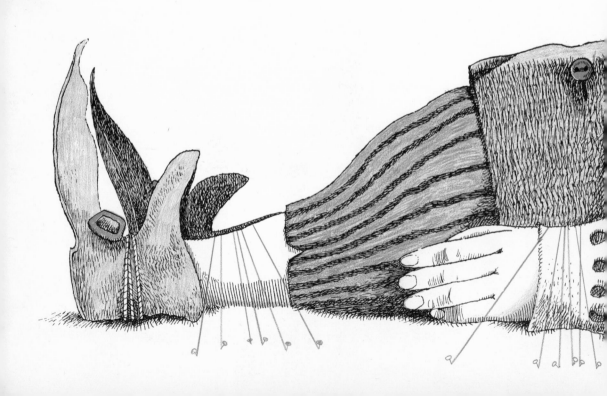

with a giant?

Would you like to try a tie on . . .

a lion?

Or would you rather be brave in the Navy . . .

even
if
it was
very
wavy?

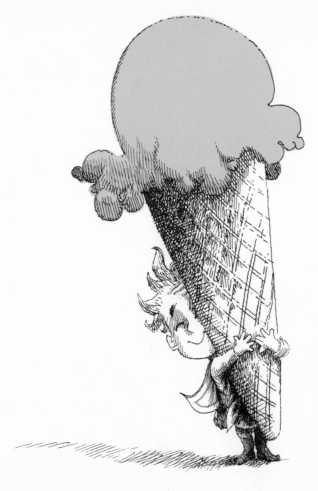

Would you like to bring home a great, big ice cream...

and hear your mother scream?

Or would you rather pay cash...

for a dashing mustache?

Would you like to write a sonnet . . .

and then spill jelly on it?

Or would you rather mail a whale...

except for the tail?

Would you like to play the whole day through...

with a pot full of glue?

Or would you rather stick with your friend...
to the very end?